Producer & International Distributor
eBookPro Publishing
www.ebook-pro.com

Tiny Light
Lee Young

Illustrations: Daria Cina

Contact: leeyoung.info@gmail.com
ISBN 9798514468539

Sleepy Kingdom

LEE YOUNG

Illustrations by DARIA CINA

That night, like so many nights before,
Noah dragged a long trail of toys he had gathered
from all across the house, and made his way into bed.
And like every night, his mother was less than pleased.

Noah hid under the covers with his
favorite stuffed animal, Teddy.

After he heard his mom's footsteps grow faint,
Noah lifted the cover and sat up straight.
He was surprised to discover that he was no longer in his
room – but far away from home, in a distant land!

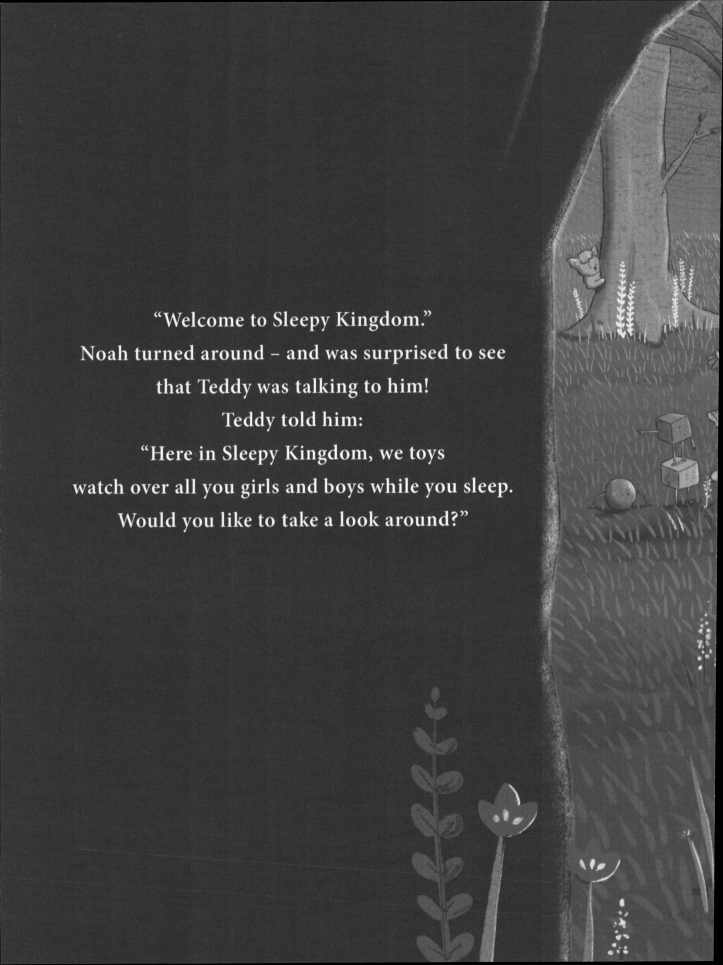

"Welcome to Sleepy Kingdom."
Noah turned around – and was surprised to see
that Teddy was talking to him!
Teddy told him:
"Here in Sleepy Kingdom, we toys
watch over all you girls and boys while you sleep.
Would you like to take a look around?"

So Teddy and Noah strolled

through Sleepy Kingdom.

They walked and walked and the further they went,
Noah felt each of his steps become slower and heavier.
He started rubbing his eyes.

"I'm tired," said Noah.

"It's time for bed. How do I get back to my room?"

"No one sleeps in Sleepy Kingdom,"
the toys' voices echoed throughout the forest.
"We all stay awake to protect the sleeping children!"

The toys weren't too pleased with Noah's plea.
They had hoped that their guest,
the only child to ever step foot in the Kingdom,
would keep them company during the sleepless night.

"Toys and games, as you must know,
I had to be in bed quite a while ago.
Come along, Teddy, it's time for us to go."

When he lifted the blanket, Sleepy Kingdom had entirely disappeared.
Noah was back in his bedroom, in his bed, with Teddy and mom,
who had come back into his room once she heard he was awake.

That night, Noah bid farewell to the toys in bed with him,
everyone except for Teddy, and with some help from his mom,
placed them all back on the shelf. So they'd still be close.

Good night.

CPSIA information can be obtained
at www.ICGtesting.com
Printed in the USA
BVHW090805121121
621193BV00004B/496